THE DRESSMAKER'S DAUGHTER

A True Story of the Holocaust

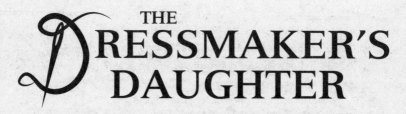

THE DRESSMAKER'S DAUGHTER

A True Story of the Holocaust

EDITH "DITTA" LOWY
with Joshua M. Greene

SCHOLASTIC INC.

ISBN 978-1-338-61941-6

10 9 8 7 6 5 4 3 2   20 21 22 23 24

Printed in the U.S.A.   40
First printing 2020

Book design by Charice Silverman

DEDICATION

In memory of my parents and dedicated to my children, Susan and Peter.

CHAPTER ONE

OCTOBER 1942— FROM ONE PERIL TO ANOTHER

MY MOTHER AND I HAD BEEN PRISONERS IN Auschwitz for two months. One dark morning, armed guards stormed into our cold, wooden barrack, pointed their rifles at us, and yelled, "You and you! Out!"

They marched us to the nearby train station,

pushed us into a cattle car crowded with other women prisoners, and slammed the doors shut. The train departed. Two days later, we arrived at another concentration camp: Stutthof. Soon after our arrival, guards pushed me and my mother onto a truck with four other women and told us we were being sent to work on a farm.

Nothing the Nazis said could be trusted. Non-Jewish prisoners might be sent to "work on a farm," but we knew what the Nazis did to Jews. They tortured and starved them. Then they killed them. Was that now going to happen to us?

Several hours later, the truck arrived at the farm—and my mother's skill as a dressmaker saved our lives.

CHAPTER TWO

THE NORMAL WORLD

I AM A SURVIVOR OF THE HOLOCAUST. I WAS A teenager during those terrible years, but now I am in my nineties and have forgotten some details of what happened to me. An important scholar of the Holocaust, Primo Levi, once wrote, "The real traumas"—meaning the most distressing events of our lives—"are the ones we don't remember." For example, I don't remember details of the cattle car that took me and my mother from our home in Vienna, Austria, to Theresienstadt, Czechoslovakia, a concentration camp 245 miles away. But I remember enough of my life during the Holocaust to tell you the story.

My name is Edith Lowy. My nickname is Ditta. The Nazi party humiliated Jews by requiring them to add an additional name—Sara for women and Israel for men—to their given name, but in private my friends still called me Ditta. I was born on February 9, 1926, an only child, and grew up with my parents, Josef and Hilda Jedlinsky.

Vienna was a beautiful city, but Austria had been on the losing side in World War I and the city had suffered. Many of Vienna's citizens lived in old, overcrowded apartment buildings with rundown outdoor toilets and no electric lighting. The postwar government improved things by building hundreds of new multistory apartment blocks with electricity, running water, indoor toilets, and playgrounds out back. My parents were not rich, but we did have our own apartment. It included a kitchen, a living room, a bedroom for my parents, and a smaller one for me.

My mother, Hilda, was a master dressmaker, one of the best in Vienna. She was always working on somebody's order for clothes. I remember the sounds of her sewing machine coming from her workshop at the back of our apartment, the whir and hum and clack-clack of the motor as she pressed harder or softer on the foot pedal that controlled the speed of the needle.

My mother could make a beautiful dress out of anything. She could take a pile of cloth of different sizes and unmatched patterns and sew them together into something spectacular. She would create dresses with such style that they looked like the most recent fashions from the finest showrooms in Vienna. She earned an outstanding reputation for the quality of her work and had many clients.

My father, Josef, was a sales representative for a leather-goods company. He traveled quite a bit and was not around as much as I would have liked. When he came back from a business trip, he always brought me presents such as a doll, a book, or a pretty box. I would have preferred that he just stay home.

My mother's mother had moved in with us, so we were four people living together, plus a house-keeper who helped wash the clothes and clean the apartment. My mother never cooked pork in our home. That was out of the question. In the Jewish religion, pigs are considered unclean and eating pork is forbidden by our dietary rules. But my mother and grandmother were excellent cooks and we enjoyed tasty meals, especially on religious holidays. I didn't consider myself particularly religious, but I did think Christmas trees were beautiful and felt sad that we never had one.

At age five I attended a kindergarten called

the Montessori School, named after the school's founder, Dr. Maria Montessori, who was an Italian educator and doctor. Montessori kindergarten was a wonderful experience for me. Everything in the classroom was designed with children in mind, including child-sized bathrooms and child-sized tables and chairs. We couldn't read yet, so the teachers gave each student a symbol to indicate which classroom items we could use. My symbol was a blue grape. The teacher used a rubber stamp to mark a blue grape on the hanger for my coat and the drawer for my pencils and books. The symbols were also stamped onto the classroom clock at different hours, so each student knew when to do certain chores.

At age six I attended the Franz Schubert Elementary School, named after a famous Austrian composer. The first year it was an all-girls school. Then the school moved next door to a bigger building, and there was a floor for boys' classes as well as a floor for girls' classes. I attended that school for four years. After that, in 1936, I went to a "gymnasium," which was equivalent to middle or high school. My parents didn't earn enough money to pay the expensive tuition, but fortunately I was able to get a scholarship. I loved learning and was excited about the future, because if I did well in the gymnasium, I might be eligible to enter college.

In the afternoons I attended Bible school. I enjoyed that, too, because there was a teacher who had a wonderful way of educating us. Instead of just reading or repeating stories, he acted them out. He pretended to be the different historical people and created voices for each of them. I remember him fondly.

So in my childhood, I was lucky to have loving parents, a nice home, sufficient food, good teachers, and fine schools. It was a happy time, and I came to expect that life would always be positive. Of course, there were sometimes problems, but I believed there would also be solutions. If you thought about a problem long enough, you could figure out a solution. For each question there was an answer. Everything made sense.

But I was wrong. When the Nazis came to power, the world stopped making sense, as my mother and I soon found out.

CHAPTER THREE

LEAVING HOME

ON MARCH 12, 1938, IN THE MIDDLE OF MY SECOND year at the gymnasium, Adolf Hitler sent his army to occupy Austria. Even as a young girl I had heard enough about Hitler to know he hated Jews and wanted to get them all out of Germany. It is too complicated to explain here why such a tyrant came to power. Part of the answer is that Germany had lost World War I. The country was in bad shape, and the German people wanted a hero to bring them out of poverty and shame. That's not the whole explanation, but by the mid-1930s most Germans thought Adolf Hitler was that hero.

Hitler's first order of business was to arrest anyone he judged to be an enemy of Germany. At first these were political opponents such as Communists and Socialists. Then he turned his attention to the Jews. Soon after, his main target was anyone who wasn't a pure-blooded German, primarily Jews, but other minorities as well such as gay people and Roma (who were sometimes called Gypsies).

Hitler's next order of business was to expand the boundaries of Germany by invading surrounding countries. "Germany needs room to grow," he insisted. I was twelve years old when my parents and I heard on our radio about the *Anschluss,* or "the joining" of Austria to Germany. The German army arrived in trucks and jeeps, with troops marching down the streets of

Austria's cities. Cheering citizens greeted the German forces and raised their arms in the Nazi salute and waved Nazi flags. Hitler arrived in my city, Vienna, on March 15, 1938. Around 200,000 people gathered to applaud their new head of state, shouting *"Heil Hitler!"* All hail Hitler.

The campaign against the Jews began the next day. Austrian antisemites—meaning people who are prejudiced against Jews and are hostile to them—rampaged through Vienna, destroying Jewish homes and beating up Jews in the streets. Events reached a climax on the night of November 9. It was called *Kristallnacht*, the "Night of Broken Glass." Rioters smashed the windows of Jewish shops, stole goods off the shelves, and set fire to synagogues and prayer houses. In less than twenty-four hours Nazi police arrested more than six thousand Jews and deported them to concentration camps.

I remember that event well. I had a girlfriend who usually came by my house to walk with me to school. The morning after *Kristallnacht,* she arrived at our door and my mother told her, "There's been trouble. There won't be any school today," and sent her home right away.

The trouble for Jews grew greater with each passing day. One day the Nazi German government passed a law forcing all Jews in German-occupied territories to wear a yellow, six-pointed cloth star on their jackets and coats. That yellow star was the symbol of the Jewish faith, and the law was another way to humiliate us. "Look," the symbol declared, "I'm a Jew." Once a man in uniform came up to me in the street. He looked at the star on my coat and yelled, "I hope they burn you soon!" Can you imagine? Here was this big guy, and I was a little girl. I was just stunned.

What surprised me most was not that some people hated Jews. That had always been going on, even in Vienna, where there was a big Jewish population that included many doctors, lawyers, and artists. What surprised me was how horribly my non-Jewish classmates began acting toward the Jewish students in our school. I remember one time when I raised my hand to answer a question asked by the teacher, and one of the non-Jewish students said to me, "What are you doing? Don't you know you're a Jew? You can't just answer a question."

The teacher did not say a word. He stood there and let it happen. I was shocked by such a hurtful change in attitude.

It wasn't just in school that people's attitude toward Jews changed. It happened in our apartment building as well. Our building housed many kinds of residents. On the lower level lived a shoemaker. On the first floor lived a husband and wife who owned a bookstore in downtown Vienna. On the second floor were some friendly retired ladies. On the third floor was a doctor. All the buildings in the neighborhood were like that, a mixture of people, Jews and non-Jews, young and old, wealthy and not so wealthy, and everyone got along fine. After the *Anschluss*, that changed. Our non-Jewish neighbors stopped talking to us and began watching our every move, looking for an excuse to report us to the police.

Then one day a stranger knocked on our door. He told us he was going to move into our apartment and that we had to leave immediately. Who was this man? How could he expect us to leave our home?

On the other hand, what could we do? If we refused, he might bring the police. They would listen to him, not to us Jews. The neighbors were not going to stop him, and they certainly weren't going to help us. We knew nothing about this person, other than he hated Jews like so many others did, and that we had no choice but to give him our apartment.

How was such a thing possible? Someone shows up at your door, tells you to leave, and you say good-bye to your home? Life was like that for Jews in those days when Nazis controlled the government.

That same day, we did as he demanded and left our apartment. We took just a few personal belongings and abandoned everything else—our clothing, furniture, books, and other possessions. We walked down the stairs and across several streets to my aunt's place. My aunt, Margarete Melzer, was a widow and lived alone in her large apartment. My father knocked on her door, and when she answered he explained what had happened. My aunt welcomed him, my mother, my grandmother, and me into her home.

Did my mother still have clients for her dresses? I can't remember. I do remember that I continued attending school, although I now had to walk there because Jews were no longer allowed to ride the buses. We weren't even allowed to sit on park benches or go to the movies.

Most everything was forbidden to Jews. Food shops could only sell food to Jews during certain hours of the day. And we had little money because Jews could no longer take their own money out of banks. Fortunately, my aunt was head nurse at a nearby hospital and earned enough to buy food for all of us.

In those days, with no warning Nazi police officers with rifles would show up in a neighborhood, grab Jews off the street, and send them away in trucks. These actions were called round-ups. That's what happened to my father in October 1939, when I was thirteen. Nazi police vans arrived on our street. Soldiers jumped out, rounded up around nine hundred Jewish men from the city, and told them they were going to be sent by train to a labor camp. No one knew what would really happen to these men. My mother and I accompanied my father to the train station and waved good-bye to him with tears in our eyes.

When we came home, I said to my mother, "I guess we'll never see him again, will we?"

"How can you say such a thing?" she said. But unfortunately, I guessed right. He never came home.

At first we did receive a few letters from my father. He had been sent to a town in Ukraine called Skala, where the Germans put him to work as a bookkeeper in a grain factory. Then the letters stopped coming, and we never knew what happened to him after that. Was my father tortured? Was he murdered? Probably, but we'll never know for sure.

My uncle was the next one to go. His situation was a little different. In 1940 he was arrested and sent to the concentration camp Buchenwald. In those days it was still possible to get released from a concentration camp if you could prove you had the right papers and enough money to leave the country for good. My aunt managed to buy a ticket for him to travel to Shanghai, China. Shanghai was one of the few places in the world that had agreed to receive Jews from Europe. She showed the ticket to the German authorities, and that was sufficient to get him released from Buchenwald.

After being released, my uncle came home and I remember thinking, "He looks scared." We lived together for several weeks, and I remember him speaking hardly at all. Whatever happened to him inside Buchenwald, now he was always afraid. If someone rang the doorbell, he jumped up and hid. He had a wound on his leg, a big frightening hole, but when I asked where he got it he didn't say a word. Out of respect for his feelings, my mother cautioned me to not ask him questions about what he'd been through.

There was a delay in getting passage to Shanghai, and before my uncle could get away, the Nazis arrested him again. This time they sent him to Treblinka, a camp built by the Nazis in a forest outside Warsaw, the capital of Poland. The Nazis built thousands of camps: concentration camps, labor camps, prisoner-of-war camps, transit camps, and killing centers called extermination camps or death camps. Treblinka was a death camp, one of the worst.

As soon as people got off the train at Treblinka, soldiers marched them directly to the gas chambers, trainload after trainload, like a conveyor belt in a factory. There was no attempt to put prisoners to work, as happened in other types of camps. There was no pretending they would have a place to live. People sent to Treblinka were immediately murdered in gas chambers. With the exception of Auschwitz, no Nazi extermination camp killed as many Jews as Treblinka: as many as two thousand people every hour.

The officers in charge of Treblinka had a strange procedure. Before they killed their prisoners, they forced them to write postcards. Perhaps they wanted to convince family members back home that the camp was harmless, but prisoners invented codes that told the real story.

For example, just before he was killed my uncle wrote us a postcard that said, "I was so pleased. I saw Otto here the other day." We knew that his friend Otto had died in Buchenwald. My uncle was writing in code, telling us good-bye, that he would be joining his deceased friend Otto soon. We never heard from my uncle again.

Sometimes people ask survivors of the Holocaust, "How could you let yourself be marched into a gas chamber? Why didn't you fight back?" First of all, we did fight back. Some Jews hid in forests and became partisans: resistance fighters who blew up Nazi supply depots and performed other acts of sabotage. Some partisan groups had hundreds of fighters, including women and children.

But it's hard to fight against tanks and machine guns. It's even harder to fight when you don't know what you're fighting. There had never been anything in history like the Holocaust. No one had ever heard of scientifically designed gas chambers or crematorium ovens.

People today who ask why Jews didn't resist have no idea what it was like. If someone comes at you quickly, you know you have to do something right away. The Nazis did things gradually, and you didn't always know how to react. First they passed laws that legally restricted Jews. For example, by law we were no longer allowed to own radios or bicycles. Next the Nazis forced Jews to quit their jobs. Then they forced Jews to move into overcrowded ghettos. Then they began sending Jews to concentration and death camps by cattle car.

The noose around our necks tightened slowly, little by little. Sometimes Jews were arrested by soldiers in the middle of the night and sent away. You woke up the next morning and found out this friend was gone, then that friend was gone, and the noose drew tighter around you and your family.

One way or another, the Nazis were determined to murder all the Jews in Europe, and there wasn't much we could do about it. In 1940 there were 200,000 Jews living in my city, Vienna. By war's end five years later, fewer than 2,000 were still alive.

CHAPTER FOUR

THERESIENSTADT, WHERE NOTHING MADE SENSE

ON A SUNDAY IN OCTOBER 1942, POLICE BANGED ON our door. They had come to take my mother away.

"We will send you to be with your husband," they said. It was obviously a lie. What did they care if my mother and father were together? It was clearly an excuse to get her to cooperate, but my mother was smart. She saw through the lie and refused to go.

"If you had wanted me to be with my husband," she told the police, "you would have arrested us together the first time. I'm not going with you." For whatever reason, these police gave up and left. My mother was one tough lady.

Then one week later, they came again. This time they didn't take no for an answer, and arrested me, my mother, my aunt, and grandmother. The police marched us to the train station, pushed us into a cattle car with a hundred or so other Jews, and sent us to concentration camp Theresienstadt.

Earlier in my story, I mentioned that the worst traumas are the ones you can't remember. I have little memory of the journey by train from Vienna to Theresienstadt. Perhaps because the fear we experienced at that moment was so great, I don't remember how long it took or what happened on the way there. I only remember that after the train arrived, guards marched my aunt and grandmother away. We had no idea where they were going or what their fate would be. Then guards made me and my mother walk from the train station to the camp.

The year before we arrived, the Nazis had transformed Theresienstadt from a military base to a concentration camp. It looked to me to be about ten blocks wide, with several streets of two- and three-story brick buildings, and the whole camp was surrounded by a barbed-wire fence. When it was a military base, Theresienstadt housed maybe seven thousand soldiers. When it became a concentration camp, the Nazis crammed more than fifty thousand prisoners into it. Every room in every building was terribly overcrowded, food was scarce, and because there was little fresh water for drinking or bathing, disease spread quickly.

Soldiers marched us into the camp through a metal gate, took away our luggage, then marched us to a two-story brick house that had formerly been an army barracks. They pushed us inside and told us to set up in the attic. We walked down dusty hallways and peered into one filthy room after another.

What we saw was like a horror show. In each room, we saw people crowded into triple-tiered bunk beds with smelly straw in place of mattresses. In one hallway, we saw something that looked like piles of old clothes that turned out to be corpses. In each room we saw people lying on the floor, sick and dying. We climbed to the attic, where we found more people sick and dying from hunger and disease. The attic had been built with old red bricks that flaked, and everything was covered with red dust. The whole house smelled vile from some kind of disinfectant.

Imagine such a scene: people lying on the ground, dying, going to the bathroom where they lay, and everything coated in red dust and smelling disgusting. We were terrified.

Two neatly dressed prisoners arrived at the house. They introduced themselves and said they had been there almost a year and were part of the Jewish Council. Council members tried to make life bearable for prisoners by securing food and medical supplies and doing other services. The Nazis allowed Jews in Theresienstadt to manage their own affairs, the two men told us, so long as the rules of the camp were respected.

While the Jews were allowed more freedom in Theresienstadt than in other concentration camps, the Nazis were just as brutal here as anywhere else, and anyone breaking the rules was severely punished. For example, there was to be no education, no classes. Anybody found teaching or having any books would be hanged.

One service the Council offered was helping young people. The two men suggested to my mother that she consider letting me live in the *Jugendheim*, the youth building, which they described as a house reserved specifically for teenage prisoners.

"Your daughter would be in a better environment there," they said, "living with other young people. And, of course, you can visit any time you want."

My mother and I talked it over and decided that if these two prisoners had survived a whole year and were still polite and well dressed, maybe they could be trusted. So we agreed. I kissed my mother good-bye and walked with the two men to the youth building.

On the way, the two men pointed out various buildings. We passed by overcrowded dormitories, supply depots, administrative offices, and warehouses where clothing and other possessions taken from arriving prisoners were sorted before being shipped to Berlin. I saw prisoners of all ages, from little kids to old people.

We arrived at the *Jugendheim*. The building was three stories tall with a slanted slate roof and high windows. Inside, the rooms were bare. There was little by way of furniture or beds, but still it was an improvement over where I had been. At least there were no dead bodies. The councilmen put me in a room with twenty or so German and Austrian girls, and it was nice to have people my age to talk to. I discovered there was a floor for boys and another for girls, and that the prisoner in charge of the boys was named Louis Lowy.

Louis was a handsome young man, six years older than me. He was in charge of about thirty boys who lived on the second floor of the *Jugendheim*. Taking care of this group of boys was Louis's main job, but he also secretly taught English and history to all the kids. Louis had spent two years in England and had dozens of stories to tell about London.

I remember one story he told about a place

called Speakers' Corner in Hyde Park, where anyone could get up on an orange crate and say anything they wanted to, about politics, the government, God, or anything else. Such freedom of speech was never permitted in Germany or any other country under Nazi control.

Louis held classes each day and taught us about the Constitution of the United States and the importance of the Preamble and the Bill of Rights. He organized literary evenings, with readings from Shakespeare and the German poet Goethe, and discussions of ideas such as "knowledge is power."

I was enchanted by him. He was passionate, intelligent, and all the children loved him. He seemed to understand that children needed affection. Many parents had been murdered by the Nazis, and he taught the other organizers in the *Jugendheim* to give the younger children special attention and reassure them that they were not alone.

Louis was bold. He even wrote out quotations from famous philosophers that we posted on our bunks to give us a sense of defiance against the Nazis, such as this quote from German playwright Friedrich Schiller: "Man is created free and is free / Even though born in chains." I appreciated Louis's notion that the Nazis had imprisoned our bodies but not our minds, and that a part of us could remain free if we never forgot that there was a larger world in which we would one day live again.

Another thing the young people did was organize theatrical productions. Putting on a play was forbidden by the Nazi administrators, and there would have been severe punishment if they found out. But when you're young you think you can take on the world.

We didn't have a real stage, so we set one up in the attic of the *Jugendheim* building. One of the boys went around the camp stealing lightbulbs and rigged up spotlights for the show. For costumes, we used whatever we could find: an old blanket, a worn-out hat, and torn pieces of fabric. The audience for our shows included prisoners from around the camp, and everyone coming to these plays was discreet and took care not to be seen going into or out of the youth house.

Louis was the director and picked a controversial play to direct, *Mary Stuart*, also written by playwright Friedrich Schiller. The play was more or less based on the life of Mary, the sixteenth-century queen of Scotland, and this play had parallels with our tragic situation inside Theresienstadt. For example, Mary is imprisoned and later executed, and there is a line one of the characters says after Mary is killed: "All enemies of this place end up like her—dead." Everyone in the audience could relate to that.

Louis gave me a part in the play, and we did several performances. It felt strange on the one hand to be suffering from disease and lack of food, and on the other hand to be putting on plays. But what better way to keep ourselves distracted from the tragedy around us than by doing something creative?

Louis was twenty-two and I was sixteen. He told me that his mother had died from dysentery just a few months earlier, and that he had buried her with his own hands. I admired him, he liked me, we enjoyed each other's company, and after a few months we began to think of ourselves as boyfriend and girlfriend, and that was a great comfort in a place where nothing was comfortable.

There were many causes of dying in Theresienstadt. Because the place was so filthy, serious disease was common. Prisoners lay on the floor suffering from scarlet fever, typhus, diphtheria, polio, and everyone was infested with lice. These little white bugs climbed over our faces at night, nested in our hair, laid eggs, and spread disease. Soon after our arrival I contracted hepatitis, which lasted for weeks.

Did the rest of the world know what was

happening to Jews in Nazi Europe? By 1943, a few prisoners had managed to escape from concentration camps in Poland and Germany. They reported about conditions in the camps to the press and to government officials in England and America. The governments did nothing to help the Jews, but months later officials from the International Red Cross announced they would make an inspection. They wanted to find out for themselves what conditions were like inside Hitler's concentration camps.

When Nazi administrators of Theresienstadt learned there would be an inspection, they took it as an opportunity to fool the world into thinking Jews lived well under Nazi rule. They forced prisoners to clean up the camp and had them build fake coffee houses. They ordered prisoners to create temporary schools and kindergartens and to plant flowers around the grounds. Then they changed the rules of the ghetto, just for the upcoming Red Cross visit, and allowed residents to borrow books from a lending library and even shop for clothes and other goods in fake stores. When these preparations were done, camp officials issued false reports to the local newspapers and radio stations that described Theresienstadt as a "spa town" where Jews were living comfortably.

The Red Cross officials were scheduled to arrive on June 23, 1944. The plan was for them to find well-dressed children playing games, painting pictures, writing poetry, and eating full plates of food. The Nazi officers of the camp insisted that while the Red Cross people were there, we children should call the Nazi officers "uncle."

Can you imagine? What a joke. The whole thing was a hoax, and we wondered whether the Red Cross officials would believe what they saw. In any case, once they left, things would certainly go back to what they had been before. We would return to being sick and hungry and watching people around us perish.

The contrast between how we usually lived and this make-believe "spa town" made me angry. I called it a "dance of death." We were allowed to decorate the ceilings of our rooms and dance around pretending to do "normal things," having a good time with all these new privileges, but it was still a concentration camp where the Nazis intended to see everyone die. It is difficult to describe how thousands of prisoners were dying, yet the cultural events went on all the same. We knew the plays and readings wouldn't last and that one day they would come for each of us, but we didn't know when that would happen.

Before the Red Cross officials arrived, Nazi camp administrators realized Theresienstadt was too overcrowded. Prisoners were practically sleeping on top of one another, and the officials knew this would not look good to representatives from the Red Cross. So, before the representatives arrived, the Nazis reduced the population of the camp by sending five thousand prisoners to Auschwitz, most of them to be killed.

My mother and I were among them. When the time came for us to leave for Auschwitz, I went to Louis, and we promised to find each other again, someday.

CHAPTER FIVE

AUSCHWITZ

THE TRAIN FROM THERESIENSTADT TO AUSCHWITZ was made up of dozens of cattle cars. Guards shoved me and my mother in with maybe a hundred other women. They slammed the door shut and locked it so no one could escape, and the train departed with a jolt. There were no windows, just open slits with no way to see out; no food and no toilet, just a small bucket that everyone had to use. On that trip, several older people in our cattle car died from exhaustion and hunger.

Finally, after several days of these horrors, the train arrived. Auschwitz was huge, the largest of the thousands of camps built by the Nazis. It took up nearly ten thousand acres of land. That's about the same size as ten thousand football fields. The Nazis opened Auschwitz in 1940, and by the time they left less than five years later, more than a million people had been murdered there. Nine out of every ten people murdered in Auschwitz were Jews.

My mother and I arrived about two miles from the main camp, at a train station called Auschwitz-Birkenau. The doors of our cattle car slammed open, and in the distance my mother and I saw long lines of barracks. Guards yelled at us to jump down from the train and line up.

A prisoner pointed to the crematorium chimneys and said to me, "You see that? That's where you are going." I remembered the small crematorium in Theresienstadt, but that was supposedly for burning bodies of people who had died from work or disease. The idea of just sending people to be killed didn't make sense to me. I was young and naïve and said, "Oh, come on. That's ridiculous."

I saw what was happening but refused to believe it. My disbelief was a self-protection mechanism. Your eyes see something unbelievable, so the mind refuses to believe it. Yet in some other part of your awareness, you know it's true.

Guards pushed me and my mother out of the line and took us to an area called "the family camp" where mothers, fathers, and children were housed together. Years later we discovered that this family camp had been inspired by Theresienstadt: a place that Nazi propagandists could point to and say, "See, families are together. It's not so bad." In reality, the family camp was no better than the rest of Auschwitz.

We lived in barracks surrounded by an electric fence and suffered like the other prisoners from hunger, cold, exhaustion, illness, and poor sanitation. The rate of people who died there was no lower than in the rest of the camp.

When we first arrived at the family camp, a woman officer looked me up and down, pointed to my feet, and said, "I want your boots." It was like the man who had kicked us out of our apartment—what was I going to do, say no? I had no choice. I took off my boots and handed them to her.

Guards marched us to a shower room where they made us take off our clothes. They herded us into a big stone room with pipes running across the ceiling. Water poured out, a few moments later the water stopped, and guards opened the doors. We hurried out of the shower room, and guards threw old clothing at us. The clothes were all sizes and shapes, and it was a good guess they had been taken off the bodies of people murdered before we arrived. I looked at the labels on the clothes shoved into my hands, and the labels were in French. "These must have been taken from murdered Jews who came from France," I thought.

Another guard shoved a pair of shoes into my hands. He didn't care whether the shoes fit or not. I remember playing a game to distract myself from the horror of our situation. I pretended I was in a shoe store. I put the shoes on, looked at them first one side, then the other, and told myself, "These shoes really don't look so good, and they're not that comfortable," as if I was thinking about buying them, instead of being in a concentration camp where there was no choice.

Days later the guards did not give us any underwear, and that was another moment when my mother's dressmaking skill proved useful. After she was pushed out of the shower, the guards had handed my mother a dress much too long for her. A few days later she managed to find a sewing needle. She ripped off a length of the hem of her dress, unraveled a long thread from the torn hem, and in just a few minutes she had sewn us panties. Having underwear may not seem like much today, but where we were, in the condition we were in, underwear was a great luxury.

When the women and girls finished putting on the clothes, we looked at one another and giggled. We looked like characters from some bizarre costume movie or dress-up parade. Everyone was so ridiculous in these ill-fitting dresses and blouses that we laughed. Then we stopped laughing because we realized that this wasn't make-believe. It wasn't a show. It was our miserable lives.

At 4:00 a.m. each day a guard stormed into our barrack and yelled for us to get up and assemble outside for roll call. This happened every day. We were made to stand at attention while guards counted every prisoner to make sure no one was missing. We stood like that without moving for hours, no matter what the weather, and anyone who was too weak to remain standing during the roll call was taken to be killed.

We learned quickly that it was better not to stand at the end of a line of prisoners during roll call. The middle was safer. Guards patrolled the lines, and if one of them wanted to kick a prisoner or hit someone with a hard stick, it was more often the people at the ends of the lines who were beaten up.

What do I remember of Auschwitz? I remember that we were afraid every minute we were there. I remember being hungry all the time. I remember not being able to wash because there was no clean water. I remember staying close to my mother every second and being terrified that the Nazi guards would separate us.

Survivors often say that unless you were actually in Auschwitz, it is impossible to understand. Imagine being in a place where, day in and day out, there is screaming and yelling, and you never know what is going to happen to you. All you know is that people are beaten and there is hardly any food, and then you die and your body becomes ashes. Nothing makes sense. Nothing is normal. Auschwitz was the opposite of normal.

One job I was forced to do was carry bricks for construction being done in the camp. My mother was not sent on that work detail with me, and every day I asked myself one question: "Will she be there in our barracks when they send us back tonight?" Conditions in the camp were so horrible that you could never predict who would survive even one day.

Many prisoners were forced out on work details in the morning and never returned. Some died from exhaustion during the work and others died from starvation. This uncertainty about your fate created unbearable fear. You just never knew what was coming next.

During our time in Auschwitz, from May to

July 1944, the government of Hungary cooperated with the Nazis by deporting around 440,000 Hungarian Jews, more than half the Jewish population of the country. Many of these Hungarian Jews were sent to Auschwitz. On a typical day three or four trains arrived, each one carrying between 3,000 and 4,000 Hungarian Jews. These poor people arrived in cattle cars the way my mother and I had arrived, but their fate was worse than ours. They were killed immediately.

My mother and I were in the camp next to where the Hungarians were being held, and we saw for ourselves that for these miserable people, it was over quickly. In less than four months, more than 380,000 Hungarian Jewish prisoners had been gassed and cremated.

My mother and I were in Auschwitz on June 6, 1944, known as D-Day, the day the Allied powers crossed the English Channel and landed on the beaches of Normandy, France. The Allies included American, French, British, and Russian troops, and D-Day was the beginning of the liberation of Western Europe from Nazi control. Within three months, the northern part of France was freed, and the American, British, and French armies were preparing to enter Germany from the west, where they would meet up with Russian forces attacking from the east. We heard rumors that the Allied invasion had taken place, and we were excited about it because we thought, "Now the war will be over!"

During our time in Auschwitz, we were tattooed on our arms. My number was A-1806. Prisoners told us that getting a tattoo with the letter A was a good thing. It meant we were young enough to be useful as workers. Instead of killing us, the Germans would send us out on a forced work detail. And that did happen. One day, a Nazi officer stormed into our barrack and pushed me and my mother and some other women and girls outside. Wherever we were being sent, we told ourselves, and whatever it was we would be forced to do, anything would be better than Auschwitz.

That was July 1944. We didn't know it then, but there were still eight more months to go until liberation.

CHAPTER SIX

STUTTHOF AND THE WITCH'S FARM

STUTTHOF CONCENTRATION CAMP WAS ANOTHER nightmare. It had been built in a secluded woody area on the northern coast of Poland. Compared to Auschwitz, it was a small camp. Still, it had a similar electrified barbed-wire fence surrounding it, and the tragedies that took place inside were just as bad. Any Stutthof prisoner judged by the guards to be too weak or too sick to work was killed. Stutthof operated from 1939 until 1945. In that time, between 63,000 and 65,000 people were killed there. About 28,000 of them were Jews.

The Stutthof camp administrators made money by renting out the prisoners as forced laborers. Some prisoners worked in equipment plants, others worked in brickyards, and some prisoners were sent to farms, which is where my mother and I ended up. It was summer, and farms needed workers to plant and harvest. A guard pushed us toward trucks that were going to a few different farms, and I quickly grabbed my mother's arm and turned to the guard.

"This woman is my mother," I told him.

My mother nodded and said, "This girl is my daughter."

Maybe because we said it in German, which not all prisoners spoke, the guard pushed us to the same truck, and we climbed on.

The truck arrived at a farm in Western Prussia owned by a nasty German woman who paid money each week to the Stutthof camp for prisoners to do whatever she told them to do. She was a tough witch who made her slave laborers work long days. Sometimes she had us clean the chicken coop, sometimes we fed her pigs, sometimes we swept up the horse and cow manure in her barn, and sometimes we worked in the fields carrying bundles of hay. We were made to work between ten and twelve hours each day. No one had a clock, but we watched the sun and knew more or less how long we had been working.

One day I was walking across the yard when a young man in uniform approached me from the opposite direction. Someone had pointed him out to me the day before and told me he was the son of the farmer, home on furlough from the German army. We passed each other, and he shouted, "Hey, you!"—an impolite way to address anyone.

I don't know if he thought I was pretty or if he was simply curious to find out who this stranger was on his mother's farm, but I refused to turn around. "He's not a guard," I told myself, "and I'm not in a concentration camp. He has no authority over me. If he wants to speak with me, let him address me like a civilized person." So I kept walking.

When the boy saw that I was refusing to acknowledge his nasty "Hey, you," he changed his tone.

"Fraulein?" he asked. That was more like it. Because he spoke politely, I stopped and turned around and looked at him.

"Yes?" I said.

"May I ask please what you are you doing here?"

"I'm a prisoner," I told him. I said it in proper German, which was unusual because not many prisoners spoke German.

"Do you mind if ask where you are from?"

"Vienna," I said, then turned and walked away. That was that. Maybe I was a prisoner, and maybe I was filthy and undernourished, but I was still a human being and deserved to be treated like one.

Besides me and my mother, officials at the Stutthof camp had also sent English prisoners of war and Russian civilian prisoners to work on this farm. The Russians were mostly strong young farm girls. My mother and I had not grown up on a farm. We were city people from Vienna and knew nothing about farm work. We were also nowhere near as physically strong as the Russian girls who had grown up doing lots of manual labor and who could carry three or four bundles of hay at a time. The English prisoners could carry two bundles of hay. We could barely carry one bundle. How could anyone expect otherwise? We had been starved for months.

The witch who owned the farm saw how weak

we were compared to the Russian girls. "You aren't working hard enough!" she yelled at my mother.

My mother put down the bundle of hay she was carrying, looked right at that woman, and said, "So pay us less!"

Everyone who heard her was shocked. What was my mother thinking, to say such a thing to someone who had the power of life and death over us? All that German woman had to do was report what my mother had said to the guards and we'd both be shot. My mother's quick comment was so unexpected that at first the witch didn't say a word. Then she grew defensive.

"What do you mean, pay you less?" she yelled back. "I'm already paying the camp enough for you people to work here." Then she sent us back to work and stomped off as though nothing had happened.

What a relief that she didn't report us to the camp administrators.

Each day after our slave labor we were locked in a cellar. There were no beds in that cellar, just a small pile of hay. There wasn't much for the prisoners to eat, nowhere near enough calories for the heavy work that we did day after day, and because I wasn't getting enough nourishment I fell sick. If the food situation didn't improve soon, I doubted I would survive.

From the starvation and hard work I developed boils, big bumps that grew on my arms and legs and caused great pain and swelling. Boils occur when bacteria get under the skin through cuts or bruises. I had a lot of cuts and bruises from working with shovels, pitchforks, wheelbarrows, and rocks, and the boils grew worse. My body did not have enough energy to cure itself of the infections. Still, in these Nazi workplaces you never told anyone you were sick. The guards would kill you rather than spend time or money nursing you back to health.

Our turn of fortune came when my mother

had the inspiration to tell the farmer that she was a dressmaker. The woman immediately realized she had someone who could be useful to her, someone who could do more than stack hay. Clothes on a farm always need repairs, and my mother was expert at mending holes in shirts and pants, sewing new garments, and making whatever else might be needed on the farm such as tablecloths or curtains.

The woman ordered guards to take us out of the cellar and put us in a heated upstairs room in her home where she kept her sewing machine. One of the English prisoners had carpentry skills, and the woman ordered him to build a wooden-framed bed for us. What a change! We were still locked in at night, but we were warm and slept in a real bed for the first time in more than two years.

Inside a concentration camp, or in our case inside a farm guarded by camp soldiers, a useful skill such as my mother's sewing ability could save your life. At least it might postpone your death. But even with such skills, you never knew when you would die. I think about other Jewish women who had dressmaking skills but who did not survive. There is no simple understanding of the Holocaust. Inside the upside-down world of the Nazi camps, there was no logic as to why things happened. What I can say is that, in our case, our lives were spared because my mother's skills proved useful to this particular woman at that particular time.

I didn't know it then, but just one month before, Louis had been deported by train from Theresienstadt to Auschwitz.

It was now the end of October 1944. Five more months until liberation.

CHAPTER SEVEN

DEATH MARCH

BY NOVEMBER OF 1944 MY MOTHER AND I HAD BEEN working on that farm for more than twelve weeks. Now that the harvest was over, we were sent back to Stutthof. There was another reason they sent us back. We had heard rumors that the Russian army was approaching from the east. Obviously the one soldier guarding the farm could not fight off the powerful Russian army. So everyone on the farm, the slave laborers as well as the man guarding us, were ordered to return to the camp.

When we arrived back in Stutthof, the other prisoners gave us nasty looks. For the past three months, my mother and I had been eating better food than what the Stutthof prisoners were given. We had been sleeping in a warm room, while Stutthof prisoners slept in freezing barracks. We were relatively healthy, while the prisoners of Stutthof continued to suffer from disease and mistreatment.

Maybe as punishment for looking better than other prisoners, my mother and I were immediately put to work digging trenches. "You're strong—go dig," was the message. This was November 1944, it was brutally cold, and digging trenches was crazy. Everybody knew the war was coming to an end. What good would trenches do? Trenches weren't going to stop the Russian army, which was arriving by aircraft as well as on foot. But then again, nothing in the camps ever made sense, so why complain?

The Russian army was coming closer every day. At night we could hear the sound of artillery in the distance. Nazi officers were relocating prisoners to Stutthof from camps farther east, and more housing was quickly needed. Camp administrators had prisoners build little round huts made of wood, stones, and whatever other scraps of material were lying around. Then they shoved maybe forty women into each hut, and my mother and I stayed in one of them through the end of December 1944.

Our life now consisted of digging trenches and getting sicker every day. My boils were getting worse and hurt like stab wounds. We had only hard, wooden-soled shoes, which made walking painful. My whole body was in agony. Whatever little bit of health my mother and I had gained working on the farm was soon lost.

We again looked like the other prisoners: walking skeletons.

By December the weather had turned even colder, and still we were forced to work every day digging ditches, wearing thin rags and with barely anything to eat. We were getting weaker, and the guards were getting more brutal. Maybe because they saw that the end of the war was near and that Hitler was losing, they beat people even harder.

In our minds, my mother and I divided the guards into "good" guards and "bad" guards. The good ones beat us less than the bad ones. On New Year's Eve 1944 we told ourselves, "Tomorrow morning will be New Year's Day. If one of the bad guards wakes us up, then 1945 will be a bad year. If one of the good guards wakes us up, then 1945 will be a better year."

The next morning, one of the good guards stormed into our hut and yelled at us to get up. We took that as a sign that 1945 would be a good year. The Russian army was approaching and soon they would defeat the Germans and liberate us from the camp.

But our troubles were not yet over. The Germans wanted to hide the crimes they had committed in the camps and did not want the Russians to find tortured and starved prisoners. So the camp officers organized a march. Anyone still alive would leave the following day for camps deeper inside Nazi Germany.

The day before the march, officers lined up all the prisoners for inspection. We knew that anyone who looked too weak for the march would be sent to the gas chamber. That probably meant us, because we were in terrible shape like so many of the others.

When our turn came, my mother and I presented ourselves to an officer, who looked us over and shook his head. We were starved and sick and could barely stand, and he pointed to his left side. We noticed that prisoners going left were marched to be killed in the gas chambers, while those who were still strong enough to walk were being sent to his right side, meaning healthy enough to go on the march.

While the officer was busy inspecting the next prisoner, my mother and I turned around and crept to the back of the inspection line. There was such disarray with the camp closing that we were able to get back into line without anyone noticing.

The second time our turn came, we approached the same folding table and the same officer was there. He didn't recognize us, but again he looked us over and pointed to his left side. My mother and I walked slowly away.

"We know what the left side means," my mother whispered to me. "We've got absolutely nothing to lose. Let's sneak back into the line again."

And so a second time we crept to the back of the line. Slowly the line moved forward. We were terrified that this time the Nazi officer would surely recognize us. But when we approached, he wasn't there anymore. He was gone, and a different officer had taken his place at the table. The new officer looked us over. Then he pointed—to the right.

That's how we survived. By chance. A stranger pointed a finger to the right instead of the left. Maybe we should have felt relief that we had been spared, but emotionally it was a low point for us. Spared for what? To walk for weeks in bitter cold, with snow on the ground and no adequate shoes, no food, and hardly enough strength to stand up?

In the morning, guards lined up all the prisoners who had been approved for the march, gave each of us a small piece of stale bread, and the march began. We walked and walked and walked. Prisoners too exhausted to walk any farther were shot. Dozens of prisoners died like that, and we stumbled past their corpses lying in the snow.

By the end of the first day we had finished our one piece of bread and were so weak it was hard to take even one more step. For two days we walked through snow and freezing wind. At the end of day two the Germans pushed us into a barn for the night. All my mother and I had was a thin smelly blanket that we'd brought with us from the camp. We huddled close together. When we woke up in the morning our blanket was gone. Someone had stolen the only thing protecting us from freezing to death. We didn't know which was worse, dying of cold or dying of hunger.

The only so-called food the guards had brought was dehydrated rotten beets. They threw a piece of it to each of the prisoners, and we took some snow or water to soften it. But that miserable piece of beet was rotten and smelly. Even though I was starving, I couldn't eat that. It was so repulsive that it made me nauseous.

The next morning we walked, and from time to

time we found ripe beets that had fallen off a farmer's wagon, and those we ate raw. That was the only so-called food there was for days at a time.

My mother and I grew weaker and weaker, and finally one night we came to the decision that it was over. We could not go on. We had heard that if you go to sleep in the snow, you freeze to death and never wake up. We just wanted it to end and agreed that in the morning we would stay there in the snow and die. Sometimes the German soldiers let people do that. But the following morning, they yelled for everyone to get up.

"Today no one stays behind!" they shouted.

So we staggered to our feet and dragged on.

Another day, another night. We were so dizzy from hunger and cold and exhaustion that we could no longer tell what direction we were headed or how many miles we had walked. Sometimes the guards themselves were so hungry and exhausted that they also had no idea where they were going, and the march went in circles.

We had been forced to walk now for a week. Most of the prisoners who had started out were dead. The remaining prisoners were barely alive and mechanically put one foot in front of the other. No one felt anything anymore. We were numb from the gnawing hunger in our bellies and the bitter cold biting into our faces.

Then one day we again arrived at a barn, and the soldiers told us to stay in the barn for the night. In the morning there were maybe twenty of us prisoners left. We all agreed that this was it. We could not go on. This time we would not get up, no matter what the guards said. We would stay behind in the snow and die. My friend Lucy got up and walked away without saying good-bye. Miraculously, she somehow survived and now lives in Israel.

The next morning, I noticed a farmer looking out of his window at us. We were like a pack of skeletons sprawled across his property. He picked up his phone and called the local authorities.

"I've got twenty or so Jews here!" I heard him shout into the phone. "I don't know what to do with them!"

The local authorities sent a truck. The driver and his helpers picked us up, shoved us into the back of the truck, and took us to another camp. This was Kokoszka, a sub-camp of Stutthof. My mother and I looked at each other, surprised to still be alive.

By the time we arrived at the Kokoszka sub-camp, my mother and I were both nauseous. We had contracted typhoid, which was a particularly nasty disease. It made you weak and constipated. It gave you headaches and skin rashes. It made you vomit, and without treatment it could kill you. But then one of the other prisoners handed us some pills. We had no idea what kind of pills they were, but we took them. How much worse could it get?

She was a nice old lady. One day she took some snow, melted it down, and cleaned the floor of the barrack. So surprising. Why she happened to have pills, and why she decided to give them to us rather than keep them for herself, will always be a mystery. I told you, nothing made sense in those days. I didn't know people were still capable of such an act of kindness. Those pills brought down our fever and saved our lives.

How to describe Kokoszka? It was a filthy mess, with Germans stationed around the periphery. As in Stutthof, we lived in a bombed-out barracks. Guards with machine guns were stationed outside. Can you imagine? None of the prisoners had the strength to stand, but still they guarded us with machine guns.

That was at the end of February 1945. We didn't

know it at the time, but there were still four more weeks till liberation.

The war was ending, no one was in charge of anything, and no one cared about Jews anyway, so we sat in that filthy mess and waited. Groups of people came and went. We didn't know who they were, but we assumed they were prisoners like us, waiting like us, hoping like us to survive another day. My mother and I couldn't move, we were so sick. Was someone going to shoot us? Were we ever going to get any food? Would we die of hunger? Of sickness?

We heard that somebody in the property next door had stolen a horse, killed it, and was handing out horse meat to prisoners. We struggled to stand up and shuffled next door. Someone was indeed handing out chopped horse meat. We took our little portion, found a stove in our barrack, and cooked it. It was food and we ate it.

The next morning I found a woman prisoner lying on the floor next to us. She was horribly sick. I heard her say, "I just want to live long enough to see my husband again." A few days later a transport of prisoners arrived, and her husband was in that group. It was the most amazing thing that she got to see him again—they were reunited. Sadly, just two days later she died. It was so disturbing.

I wanted to survive. I wanted to be clean again, to wear washed clothes, to sit in a beautifully decorated room and eat a fresh roll and drink a cup of hot cocoa. I remember dreaming of such a future through my delirium. "I don't want to die now," I mumbled. The hunger and exhaustion were overwhelming now. "The war is almost over," I told myself. "I want to live." The last thing I saw before falling unconscious was a big German machine gun pointed at us.

None of us knew there was only one more day till liberation.

CHAPTER EIGHT

LIBERATION

THE MORNING WE WERE SUPPOSED TO DIE WE WOKE up, and the Nazi soldiers were gone. The big German machine guns were gone as well. In its place was a new machine gun. This one was Russian. We came out of our bombed-out house and saw Russian troops swarming everywhere. The Russian army was closing in, and the Nazis were on the run. The date was March 21, 1945.

I call it my renaissance birthday—the day I was reborn, liberated.

My mother and I were among the few prisoners who had survived the journey from Stutthof to the Kokoszka sub-camp. One of the other women survivors spoke Russian and told us that the Russians planned to take us to Danzig, a city two hours away on the edge of the Baltic Sea. From there, they said we could make our way home to wherever we came from. My mother and I could barely imagine what it would be like to go home to Vienna. What would we find there after so long?

We stayed and ate food provided by the Russians. When we were a bit stronger, we climbed into one of the Russian trucks and were driven two hours to Danzig. When we arrived, we could barely believe our eyes. The Russian army had successfully defeated the Germans, but in the process they had completely destroyed the city. There were hardly any buildings left standing.

The city was like a pretend stage set in a movie, where you saw the fronts of houses but nothing behind them. Everything was wrecked. The buildings lay in ruins. Whatever trees once lined the streets had been burned to the ground. To walk anywhere we had to climb over rubble, bricks, and broken furniture.

The Russian officials taking care of returning survivors assigned a bombed-out house to each of the women from Kokoschka. My mother and I were taken to the mayor's house, which was one of the few houses still partially standing. It had been bombed like the other houses, but there were enough rooms still intact that the Russians turned the house into a hospital with a few rooms for survivors including me, my mother, and six Hungarian girls. It was there that we ate our first real meal in longer than I could remember.

By the beginning of May 1945, all German troops had surrendered, not only in Germany but also in Italy, the Netherlands, and other countries they had conquered during the war. Victory in Europe was at last declared by the Allies on May 7, 1945. Some Russian soldiers handed me and my mother glasses of vodka and toasted us.

I will never forget this one incident. A young Russian soldier was patrolling near where we stayed. He looked so young, maybe a teenager, and he spoke a little English and so did I. He looked at me for a while with this soft expression on his face and said, "I have a little sister about your age." Then he handed me a slice of bread and continued on his patrol. I never saw him again, but for just that moment we were not Russian or Austrian. We were not friends or enemies. We were two young human beings.

The next day, the Russian officer in charge wrote up travel documents on little slips of paper and gave them to me and my mother. Those slips of paper were all we had to get us home. We had no other papers, no student cards, no driver's license, no work permits, no nothing. Everything had been taken away from us years ago. Those two little pieces of paper were our entire identities.

On the train I met a Polish engineer who spoke German. He told me, "Many of the bridges have been destroyed. If you want to get to Vienna, first take the train to this town, then that town. Then get another train and go to this other town, then the town after that, and then head west. Then you can get to Vienna."

I memorized what he said, but we had no idea if we would ever get to Vienna.

"Just don't speak German," he told me. "The conductor will think you're a Nazi and throw you off the train." How crazy was that!

The next morning before leaving I went to say good-bye to the six Hungarian girls. My mother and I were going west. The girls wanted to go east, back to Hungary, but they had not been given any identity papers.

"Would you give us one of your two papers?" one of them asked me.

I wanted to help. I wanted to do something nice for somebody, like the woman who had given us the pills to cure our typhus. I thought if the six girls had at least one identity paper between them maybe that would be enough to get them home. So I gave them mine.

When my mother found out, she was furious. "How can you go anywhere if you don't have your identity paper?"

"Mom," I said, "it means nothing. It's a piece of paper. We have yours. We'll be fine."

Finally, Russian soldiers put us on a train and we left. Travel was free at that time, so we didn't worry about buying tickets. I don't remember everything about that journey home. I do recall that at one stop Russian doctors made us take a bath because we were so filthy. And because our heads were infected with lice, they cut off all our hair.

The train stopped in Bratislava. At that time it was in the easternmost part of Czechoslovakia.

We stepped down from the train and saw a conductor.

"Where is the connecting train to Vienna?" I asked him.

"There is no connecting train to Vienna," he said. "All the bridges have been bombed."

We had no choice but to stay in Bratislava during all of May and June 1945, waiting for a train to take us home. We had no money and at first no place to stay.

Then, once again, my mother's dressmaking skills saved us. We met a woman who lived in a large apartment. Her mother had been deported and her husband was in prison for having collaborated with the Nazis. She lived alone with her three-year-old son. Somehow, she had managed to acquire huge piles of fabric. When she learned my mother could sew, she took us to live with her and kept my mother busy creating clothes.

Eventually we found a Russian truck driver willing to take us to Vienna. We said good-bye to the woman with the stacks of cloth, climbed into the truck, and headed out of Bratislava. Two hours later we arrived back in Vienna. We were home after nearly three years in hell. The truck driver kissed my hand, then my mother's hand, wished us good luck, and drove off.

Immediately we walked to our apartment building and asked the super to open the door to our former apartment. We climbed the stairs, and he opened the door. The man who had forced us to leave was gone. Gone as well were all our clothes, books, and furniture. It was just an empty, dirty apartment with papers scattered across the floor, dust on the shelves, and nothing from our former life.

Unfortunately the super wasn't so generous as to let us move back in with no money, but we couldn't face living there again anyway. The memories of growing up there were too painful. We couldn't bear the thought of trying to rebuild something that didn't exist anymore. We closed the door and walked down the stairs.

Someone told us there was a Jewish Central Committee set up to help survivors returning to Vienna. We walked to the address and registered our names, just in case anybody came through looking for us. Then we set out to find our family.

First we got a ride back to Bratislava, where one day we saw a woman on the street, wearing a dress that had belonged to my grandmother. We knew it was my grandmother's because it was my mother who had made it for her and the details were unique to my mother's creations. We approached this woman and asked her where she got the dress.

"Theresienstadt," she said.

Without thinking twice, I said to my mother, "We have to go back to Theresienstadt. Maybe grandma is still alive. We have to try to find her."

In my mind I was also thinking maybe we would find my aunt—and my boyfriend, Louis.

It was a long route that next took us to Prague, where we again went to the local Jewish Central Committee office. "Is there any way to get to Theresienstadt?" we asked.

A girl I had once known happened to be there and overheard us. She walked over and said, "I'm going there. You can ride with me."

Together we rode back to Theresienstadt. At the main office, which was now occupied by friendly American and Russian soldiers, an office worker checked the files.

"I'm very sorry," he said to me. "Your grandmother died a month ago. She lived long enough to see the liberation and the end of the war."

Then he informed us that my aunt had been shipped out to Auschwitz in September 1944 and killed.

"Do you have any information about Louis Lowy?" I asked. He checked his files.

"Yes, Louis was here," the officer told me. "He has gone to the Displaced Persons camp in Deggendorf, Germany."

"How can I get a message to him?" I begged the office worker.

"You're in luck," he said. "There is someone here who happens to be going there. Maybe he will bring the note for you."

He found the person, and it turned out to be a boy I had known in Theresienstadt named Heinz Berger.

"Please do me a favor," I asked him. "Take a letter from me and give it to Louis."

I later learned that Heinz delivered my letter to Louis, who read it and screamed, "My God! Ditta is alive? Where did you see her?"

"I met her at the Jewish Cultural Center," Heinz said. "She was there with her mother. They are living in Bratislava."

"I'm going there—right now," Louis told him.

He changed into nicer clothes, jumped on a

truck that took him to a train, and eventually he arrived at our address in Bratislava. I had just come home and was in my room. My mother came in and said, "Louis is here."

I couldn't believe my ears and didn't know what to say. "What does he look like?" was the best I could do.

"Oh," my mother said, pretending to be casual about it, "very nice. He's dressed up in a suit and tie." She gave me a mischievous smile. A suit and tie? I'd never seen him dressed like that.

I went into the other room, and Louis and I just stared at each other.

"I'm taking you and your mother back to Deggendorf," he finally said. "To the DP camp. Today."

CHAPTER NINE

DISPLACED PERSONS CAMP

LOUIS DESCRIBED FOR ME THAT HE HAD SURVIVED IN Auschwitz by caring for his friend, Vern, whom he had met in Theresienstadt. Louis had always been like that, living to provide for others. Louis and Vern were together in the same barracks and were assigned to the same work detail, rebuilding a factory thirty miles away. Together they dug ditches, leveled the ground with their shovels, and worked in subzero temperatures without adequate food or clothing. Then, because Louis spoke German so well, he was transferred to a desk job indoors, where he was able to stay warm and eat slightly better food.

With the approach of the Russian army, Louis and Vern were sent on a death march just as my mother and I had been. And just like us, one morning Louis, Vern, and a few other friends from the camp awoke to find the Germans had run away. With his ability to speak four languages, Louis became the group leader. At twenty-four, he was also the oldest and the most daring. He managed to get his group onto a coal train that traveled east.

They traveled farther and farther into Poland, by train and on foot, finding blankets, tins of food, and even books along the way. Eventually, the group decided the best place to go was back to Theresienstadt. They hoped, as my mother and I had, to find friends or family still alive.

They found no one. Soon the American forces announced plans to open a Displaced Persons camp in Deggendorf and invited Louis to be the head organizer.

For Jews and other survivors of the Holocaust, the end of World War II brought new challenges. Many had lost their families in concentration camps, others had lost their homes in bombings, and it was difficult to get the papers needed to immigrate to another country. So many survivors had no choice but to move into Displaced Persons camps in Germany, Austria, and Italy. These DP camps, as they were called, existed from 1945 to 1952, when the last one was closed.

Deggendorf was a medium-sized DP camp in the American zone, meaning that large area of Germany liberated by the American army. Big DP camps housed as many as twelve thousand people. Deggendorf started with five hundred people, then another three hundred people arrived from Theresienstadt. Previously the camp had housed a military school, and the buildings were big concrete structures. Survivors took advantage of the facilities to re-create some of the life they had known before it was destroyed by Hitler and his Nazi murderers. They built schools, started sports clubs, began farming projects, performed music, staged plays, and initiated other community activities.

My mother and I arrived with Louis on November 1, 1945. It didn't surprise me to find that Louis was co-director of the whole place. Organizing people was what he had done in Theresienstadt, and he was a natural leader. He also spoke perfect English and that was important, because the DP camp was set up in the American zone.

Louis assembled a team of helpers, and together they built the DP camp into a thriving community. Everyone was enthusiastic to help. They had lost their families, their homes, their belongings. The Nazis had even taken away their names and replaced them with numbers. Here at last was a chance to rebuild their lives.

Louis studied the list of people and matched their skills with jobs to be done. They set up departments of housing, food, education, and culture. They set up a court system that included lawyers who had survived the camps. The camp had two newspapers, a library, a synagogue, a kosher kitchen, and printed its own paper currency. There was even a swimming pool in Deggendorf.

Louis and his team put their heads together and came up with solutions to the problems of creating an entire self-sufficient town. They opened a home for the aged. They organized lectures, poetry readings, a kindergarten, adult-education courses, a hospital, a movie theater, a football field. And most important, they established a democratic system of self-government. They chose their own leaders through free elections, the opposite of the oppressive, murderous dictatorship of the Nazis.

Louis was super smart, a real genius in my opinion, and invented ways to keep people optimistic about the future. One way was by having everyone in the camp fill out forms saying what country they'd like to live in. Most of them wanted to go the United States. One day we learned that the Americans had opened a consulate in Munich, Germany, a two-hour drive away. That was good news, because visas to go to America were issued by the consulate. Louis translated into English the forms that people in the camp had filled out—more than two hundred of them—then he traveled to Munich, submitted the forms, and succeeded in getting visas.

Smart, kind, and good looking. What more could a girl want in a husband? We were married one month later, in December 1945. I tell people we were never engaged because technically he never asked, "Will you marry me?" What he said was, "The director of the DP camp is leaving, but he wants to be the best man at our wedding. We have to get married before he leaves."

Not very romantic, but you can't have everything. Naturally, my mother made my dress. It was gorgeous.

By early May 1946, the first steamship was ready to leave Bremerhaven, Germany, to bring survivors to New York. My mother received her visa first, so she boarded the first steamship, called the *Marine Perch*, and departed for America without me. Throughout the war we had never been separated, so you can imagine how traumatic it was to be apart now, for the first time in my life.

Fortunately, soon after my mother left, we learned that a second ship, called the *Marine Flasher*, would soon be departing from Germany. Louis and I boarded in late May.

Eight days later, we arrived in America.

CHAPTER TEN

AMERICA

"WHAT WAS IT LIKE ARRIVING IN AMERICA AFTER THE Holocaust?" I get asked that question a lot. There were many good things, such as seeing the Statue of Liberty as our ship arrived in New York Harbor, and reuniting with my mom, who was living with her sister-in-law in Boston. I could also tell you how shocked I was seeing hundreds of pairs of shoes in a store window. I had never seen so many shoes. Just one pair of shoes in Auschwitz was like gold.

I could tell you about the jobs Louis and I found after coming here, he as a bookkeeper and me working in a factory. I could tell you how Louis earned a master's degree in social work and then eventually a PhD from Harvard and became a well-respected professor. I could tell you about how I went back to school and also earned a degree in social work. I could tell you that we had two wonderful children, Susan and Peter. As important as those events were for me, there were some sad moments I'd like to mention to you.

The greatest loss was when my mother died just two years after arriving in America. I thought about how bravely she fought to survive and how sad that she enjoyed only two years of freedom here. I thought about the wonderful relationship we had and how much we had been through together. During the war we were more like sisters than mother and daughter. I would have liked more time with her, so we could become mother and daughter again.

My husband, Louis, died in 1991. Of course, I miss him terribly, but he and I had a full life in America. We were married forty-six years, and when he died he was seventy-one. My mother was only fifty-two. She died too soon.

The biggest surprise since coming here was discovering how many people know nothing about the Holocaust. Even today, it still surprises me. Somebody asked me recently, "Did they serve desserts in the camps?" Another person asked, "What did you do on weekends in Auschwitz?" Another person once asked, "When did you decide to leave Auschwitz? Who made the travel plans?" I suppose it's understandable that people want to apply terms of normal life to the Holocaust, but it doesn't work.

So how to answer the question, "What was it like arriving in America after the Holocaust?" For those of us who went through the Holocaust, there is no "after." The memories are still very much alive. Because I'm writing about it today, I know I'll dream about it tonight and have night-mares again about what I went through. The nightmares are one consequence.

Another consequence is called *separation anxiety.* That's the term in psychology to describe the fear of being left alone. I think the first time I felt it was when my mother sailed to America without me. I was an only child, so the anxiety might have been greater for me. Still, even today I become anxious when I'm separated from someone or left out. For instance, I can be stand-ing in line for a movie. I get to the box office and the ticket seller tells me, "The film is sold out." No big deal. A normal person would think, "Okay, I won't see it today. I'll just go home and see the movie another day."

Not me. I stand there afraid because somebody in authority said to me, "The others can come in, but not you." Even that can trigger separation anxiety.

So what lesson can I offer you from my experiences? Maybe the best answer I can give is this: Study, learn, and never stop learning. The history of humanity is one of constant learning—learn how to live a civilized life, learn from the mistakes of the past, learn to recognize the symptoms of tyranny and how to address them before it is too late.

That is the part of my Jewish heritage that I admire most: the love of knowledge. Knowledge is not boring. When taught by inspired educators, knowledge is exciting and an adventure. And the highest form of knowledge is self-knowledge, a better understanding of ourselves and what makes us human.

If I have learned anything from the Holocaust, it is that when we turn away from our better selves, as did those people who followed Hitler, we can fall far and commit unspeakable crimes. But when we turn toward our better selves, we humans can achieve great things. My dear Louis was like that, someone who always tried to be the best human being he could be, and who tried to help others be the best they could be.

Someone asked him, "How can you tolerate those people who did those horrible things to you?" Louis's reply has been a kind of guiding light for me and for many others.

"People do bad things," he said. "If we want people to do better, we have to teach them how."

EPILOGUE

THE WORD *HOLOCAUST* IS GREEK FOR "BURNT offering." In ancient Greece, priests burned animals as sacrifices in ritual fires. During World War II, Germany's Nazi government burned not animals but the Jewish people. Since then the word *Holocaust* has referred to the mass murder of Jews in Nazi-occupied Europe.

Why the Nazis specifically murdered Jews is difficult to explain. Throughout the ages, Jews have been unjustly blamed for many things, for which they have suffered different degrees of persecution. The Holocaust was the most extreme. More than six million Jewish men, women, and children were killed. Millions of non-Jews were also murdered by the Nazis, but Jews were the only people targeted for total extermination. The Holocaust was the systematic, state-sponsored, scientifically designed destruction of all the Jews in Europe. We know now that if Hitler had won the war, his plan was to murder every Jew in the world.

How do we even begin to understand that? What happens to some people, that they become so afraid of others they want to destroy them all? And what happens to other people, that they are so compassionate that they are prepared to sacrifice their own life for the sake of others?

It's quite a mystery and hard to solve. Still, we have to try. You have to try.

That's why I've told you my story.